E
Br

741083

11.95

Brown
If at first you do not see

DATE DUE

MAR 03 2004			
M3	S 8	24	
03	6		
0-9	21	N-21	7
I-12	10		
m3	10	5690	9
0-4-90 60		0-19-90	6
T-8			
2-795	H44	6	
FEB 26 1990			
MAR 17 1997		APR 0 4 1997	

GAYLORD 234   PRINTED IN U. S. A.

DISCARDED

For Ken

Copyright © 1982 by Ruth Brown
All rights reserved, including the right to reproduce this
book or portions thereof in any form.
First published in the United States in 1983 by
Holt, Rinehart and Winston, 383 Madison Avenue,
New York, New York 10017.
Published simultaneously in Canada by Holt, Rinehart and
Winston of Canada, Limited.
Originally published in Great Britain
by Andersen Press Ltd.

Library of Congress Cataloging in Publication Data

Brown, Ruth.
If at first you do not see.

Summary: A caterpillar has some scary adventures
before becoming a beautiful butterfly. The reader
needs to turn the book as he reads as there is
writing around the sides of the pages.
[1. Caterpillars—Fiction.
2. Metamorphosis—Fiction] I. Title.
PZ7.B81698If 1983   [E]   82-15527
ISBN: 0-03-063521-7
First American Edition
Printed in Great Britain
1 3 5 7 9 10 8 6 4 2

ISBN 0-03-063521-7

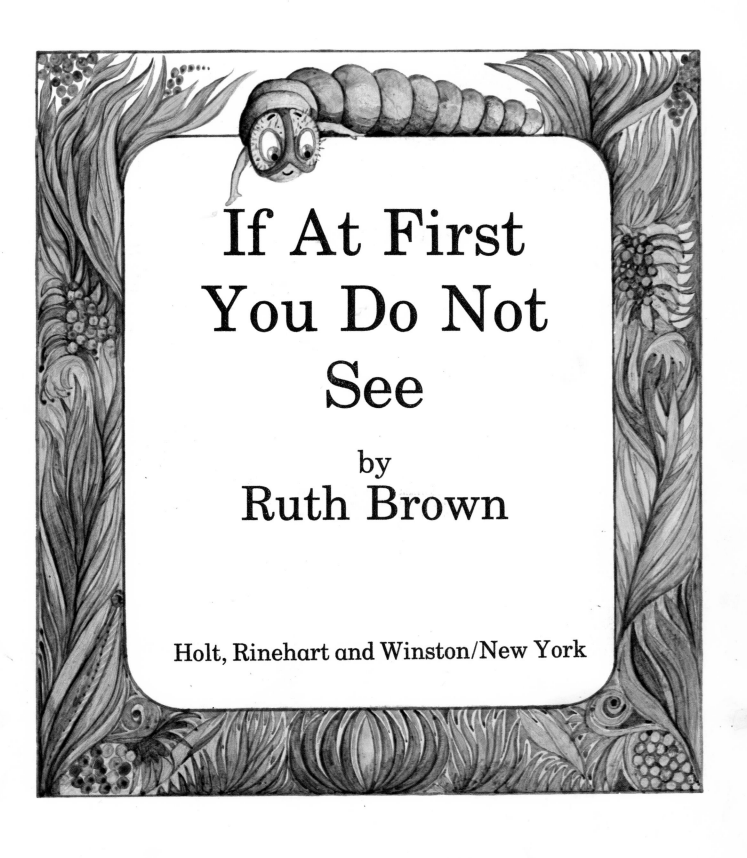

If At First You Do Not See

by
Ruth Brown

Holt, Rinehart and Winston/New York

"Now   stay here and eat those leaves,"
said the butterfly to her caterpillars.

"Ugh! How boring," said one caterpillar.
"I want something more appetizing. I'm leaving. . . ."

"Oops! Sorry!" said the caterpillar as he crawled away.

"That looks a bit more juicy," said the caterpilla

caterpillar. "Where are you?"

said a voice. "You're eating my hair!" "What?" said the

as he started to nibble . . . "Ouch! Get off!"

"Oh dear! I'm v-v-very sorry, sir."

And he very quickly climbed off the giant's face.

"Look at that lovely clump of grass . . ."

"Wha-a-a-t?" said the caterpillar.

"Get off my nose, you nasty, green worm," a voice boomed.

I think I'll taste it," said the caterpillar.

saw the two funny men. "But I'm so hungry —

and I can't seem to find anything to eat."

"Mmm . . . delicious ice cream.

"Get off! Go away!" said two squeaky voices.

I'll have some of that," said the caterpillar.

I think I'll get away from here . . . quickly!"

"Oh, look! A delicious mushroom!

But I'll just have a look to make sure it's safe.

That definitely looks good enough to eat.

"Touch me and I'll feed you to my pretty bats."

"Aaaaah!" screamed the caterpillar as he ran away.

"Yum, yum, tasty flowers," said

you miserable little grub.

hissed a voice. "How dare you mistake me for stupid flowers,

the caterpillar. "Flowerssss, flowerssss,"

"Pardon me, I'm sure," said the caterpillar.

"You're too ugly to eat anyway," he shouted as he ran away.

"Oh! This is more like it — two juicy hamburgers!"

said the caterpillar. "I'm hungry enough to eat both."

"Hey! Get off, you horrible little creepy-crawly," said a deep

voice. "Yeah – go away," agreed a second.

the poor little caterpillar was fast, fast asleep.

"I'm starving, lonely, and exhausted," cried the

"Let's have a look at you, little fella."

"What are you doing up there?" said a husky voice.

caterpillar. "I'll just have to rest in this straw."

"You poor little thing," said the scarecrow.

"I'll put you in my pocket. You'll be safe there."

It's just a field of leeks.

Aren't I a silly creature to be frightened of that!"

When he awoke he fell to the ground.

"I've got to get away from them as quickly as possible.

"Yikes! Look at those fierce looking men!" he cried.

that he had become a beautiful butterfly.

"Oh no! Another ugly monster! Hel-l-lp!"

"I'm just the same as you."

"Who are you calling an ugly monster?"

"Just a minute," said the creature.

The butterflies said good-bye to the scarecrow

that the whole world smiled.

They looked so beautiful and happy

and flew high up into the sky.